HE SAID CAREFUL… HE LIED!

Deception: He Lied Miniseries

Book 3

Daphne Dennis

TLM Publishing House

Copyright

Social Stamina – 1,2,3 Let's Go!

Titles to help look at things from other perspectives and strengthen your mindset.

The Great Ascension–1,2,3 Let's Go!

Titles to help you gain focus and climb the ladder of success!

How to Start – 1,2,3 Let's Go!

Titles to help you with step-by-step, must-have knowledge of the business world and personal experiences.

Top 10 Questions to Ask Before You…1,2,3 Let's Go!

Titles with must-have questions (and logic behind) for many of life's daily and major decisions.

Find our fiction below!

https://www.ttpublishinghouse.com/legendsreborn

https://www.ttpublishinghouse.com/7wishes

https://www.ttpublishinghouse.com/mallcadet

Social Media

Facebook: tlmpublishinghouse

Website: www.TTpublishinghouse.com

Want to Read for Free?

You may qualify for a spot on our Advance Reader Copy group.

Never heard of an ARC Group?

Simply put, it's a small group of people who are interested in a specific genre and are invited to read books before they're published.

Your feedback can help alter the storyline or even catch an elusive typo!

You're asked to provide an honest review when it is published, and that's it!

You read for free!

Go now to confirm your interest in the ARC Group!
https://www.ttpublishinghouse.com/joinTLMarc

Contents

Black

Debbie held the Maltese Poodle that was on her lap, petting his fluffy white fur as she gazed at the pool, which had a layer of dead leaves. “You’re the only one who understands me now, Fluffy, the only friend I have left.” The dog barked. “What? Best friends, really? Of course, I’ll be your best friend.

We’d better go back in the house, though. I don’t want you to drown.” Fluffy barked three times in a row. “No, Fluffy, now is not a good time for me to teach you how to swim. I have other things on my mind right now.” Debbie kept replaying the scene over and over again in her head of how she had found Herman’s body.

She had thought for sure that he was the murderer. What had Judy and Herman gotten mixed up with? What was even worse was the realization that her estranged husband, Ed, was somehow caught up in all of this, too. It did not sit right with her that she might one day find the man's body somewhere, lifeless, pale and-

She sighed as she shook all over. Debbie went back into her house with Fluffy trailing behind her. The backyard was a stark reminder of how alone she was. It was a place full of nostalgia, reminding her of swimming with the kids and late-night cookouts. *No one ever tells you that your kids are going to grow up.*

Even though she and Ed were separated, he was still her husband, and it would be heartbreaking to find him in the state she had found Judy and Herman. But what if the killer had already gone after Ed? It had been a while since she'd last seen him.

Would that mean that the next target is... me?

Debbie's mind went blank for a second. How she wished she could escape this situation. She sat down in her dining room, surrounded by the purple walls. A gallery of paintings and photographs had been erected on the walls to give the space some personality.

It contained a replica of "The Starry Night" by Vincent van Gogh, Debbie's favorite of his masterpieces. *Why did I paint these walls purple?* She thought. *It doesn't suit my mood anymore. I should have painted them black.*

"I have to figure out where those papers are, Fluffy," she said to the dog. "*You* don't happen to know where they are, do you?" Fluffy barked. "No? Too bad."

They seemed to be the link to everything that was happening. The 50-year-old with shoulder-length, blonde hair tried to look under every nook and cranny of her house, every gap between furniture or portraits that Judy might've slipped the papers behind. Sadly, she had no idea where they could be.

Still completely distraught, Debbie jumped and shrieked in surprise when her phone rang and broke the silence. Scrambling towards it in a panic, thinking that it was the killer finally catching up to her, she sighed in relief when she realized that it was her mother, who still had no clue what she was going through, as usual.

She was more concerned with her own agenda.

Debbie took a moment to even her breathing before picking up the call. "Hello? Mom?"

"What took you so long to answer?" Debbie rolled her eyes as she grunted exasperatedly.

"I was cleaning the house." She lied.

"Oh? Finally getting rid of those hideous trinkets I told you to toss? I'm guessing you got them at some sort of garage sale."

"Mom, please. If you have nothing else to say, I'm really busy, so I should go back to what I was doing."

"Is that any way to treat your mother, Deborah?" She asked before continuing. "I called because I'm having a party, and I need you to come."

Her mother wanted Craig to attend, but the man refused unless Debbie was going as well. She met Craig once, and that had been enough. She didn't mind his bald head and glasses so much. *It was the way he talked, or the things he talked about, or both, maybe*. Debbie certainly didn't want to go to a party, not when her mind was already preoccupied with the unsolved case.

"I'm sorry, mom, I can't go. I have too much housework I have to do," Debbie answered. "And... I have to clean the pool."

"Why don't you have your pool man do it?" Her mom asked.

"I don't have a pool, man." Replied Debbie.

"Okay, I'll send over mine."

"The truth is, I can't go to the party because I don't want to go to the party." *It feels good, to be honest.*

At that, Debbie's mother hung up on her. *Okay, well, that doesn't feel good.* "Bye, mom," she said to the air. "It was nice to talk to you. Have a wonderful day too." Frustrating as that was, she chose not to think about it too much as she continued to focus her attention on the cryptic case.

Debbie took her usual route to work. She was able to see the ocean from the top of the hills, its glorious waves crashing into the sand. After 10 minutes, she arrived at the vineyard where she worked; it had a sleek modern design with masculine tones, making it the perfect place to enjoy some of the greatest wine in the world. Lawn games and al fresco wine service was available in the open grassy area. Debbie exited her car. *I hate lawn games, they should outlaw them.*

Once Debbie arrived at the winery, Patty, a pretty brunette in her 50s, smiled profusely when she saw her. "Debbie! Hey! Did you know that your mom invited me to a party? Isn't that great!?" she squealed in excitement, her eyes twinkling.

Patty had always been an enthusiastic person, but Debbie still didn't understand why she would want to go. The last party had been a total failure. She had thought there would have been a lot of people there, but there was only one. It was just like her mom to trick her like that, trying to set her up with such a boring, tedious man as Craig.

"You sound so thrilled," Debbie noted as Patty nodded animatedly before clasping both hands together with a dreamy sigh.

"There will surely be lots of eligible *men* there. What are the odds that I might finally find the one?"

Debbie resisted the urge to roll her eyes at her friend, who was a hopeless romantic. "I doubt there will be. Why are you so interested in men? I hate men. They make you fall for them and end up leaving you without explanation."

"Hey, come on. Not all of them are like that. Besides, aren't you interested too?"

"Not anymore, and I'm not going."

"Huh? Wait, why?" Patty asked, eyebrows furrowed. "You're not going to your own mother's party?"

"I just don't feel like it. And, if I were you, I would drop that fantasy of ever meeting a great man at a party, especially if it's my mom's party. God forbid. Men can be very disappointing." Debbie frowned.

To her credit, Patty truly was determined to have Debbie come with her to the party. And although Debbie could say no to her own mom, she couldn't say no to Patty.

"Fine. Okay, we'll go. Patty, how can you be so persistent? I hate you, by the way...."

Debbie said sarcastically, half-bewildered and half-amused by her friend. Patty threw her arms around her for a bone-crushing hug, squealing like a giddy teenage girl.

So, that was that. Her fate was sealed, she was going to another dreadful party organized by her mom. *Oh, joy.*

After a long day of work, Debbie finally arrived home. It was a spacious, two-story, three-bedroom home with sleek lines and contemporary décor. *This house is way too big for one person*, she thought as she entered the dusty home.

Debbie went upstairs to get ready for the party. The design of the bedroom created a relaxing ambiance, with a neutral color palette and bay windows. *I should paint this room black too*, Debbie thought. She had a few cosmetics on her vanity table along with her jewelry box and some clothes to choose from laid flat on her bed.

She tried on a few sets of clothes. After a few changes, she still couldn't find the perfect fit until she glimpsed at a box that was peeking over the top shelf of her closet. Reaching for it on her tippy toes, she gasped when the contents spilled out on her. As she stepped on a silky top, she fell butt first with a loud thud, a red dress casually covering half her vision.

"Ouch."

She winced, rubbing her sore back before taking the dress off her head. She examined the dress, rummaging through her brain to remember exactly why and how she had gotten it. *Maybe for the children's graduation? Or a reunion? Or a date? No, no.*

The last one was too far-fetched to even count as an option. She couldn't even remember if she'd worn this one before. Debbie rose, stretching out her hand to fully inspect the dress. It was semi-formal with a low v-cut neck, 3/4 sleeves, and a pencil skirt-styled bottom that had a little slit stopping just short of midway up her thigh. It was a little revealing, actually, but it was too pretty not to try on. She looked drop-dead amazing with it on, and, despite her age, the dress fit her perfectly. Without wasting any more time, Debbie finished getting ready and drove to the party.

However, as soon as she parked her red sedan on the street of her mother's house, her mood darkened again. Though it was too late to drive back home, she was tempted. She moved to turn the engine off but stopped as she heard a loud honking sound coming from behind her car.

She turned her engine off, glancing at the side-view mirror to see Patty already making her way towards the car. Debbie momentarily closed her eyes, gathering all of her will so that she could be calm throughout the party, before hearing a gentle knock on the car door. Patty's muffled voice could be heard through the window as she saw her gesture for her to finally come out of the car. Hesitantly, Debbie obliged.

"Look at you! So gorgeous! I didn't know you owned a dress like that." Patty said with a big grin, putting up two thumbs. Debbie laughed softly, rolling her eyes playfully at her before smiling.

"You look pretty yourself. Did you just buy that dress for the occasion?" Patty nodded, doing a full 360 for Debbie. She looked pretty indeed. That light pink dress certainly suited her.

After exchanging compliments, the two decided to enter the house. Patty stared once again at the enormous spiral staircase that appeared to go up to heaven. The second-floor gallery had polished wood floors with an ornate railing; a Persian rug covered the floor.

"I still can't get over the fact that you grew up in this house," Patty said.

"It was a prison," Debbie replied.

"I wish I'd grown up in this prison."

"You know what would be a great color for this place?" Debbie asked.

"What?"

"Black."

Debbie's mom caught sight of them as she made her way to the door. The house had changed little since Debbie had lived there, looking eerily the same aside from a few added artifacts carefully placed on a three-story mahogany shelf in the corner of the living room.

It brought back memories for Debbie as soon as she stepped inside, the familiar bland beige walls, the ever so spotless golden-oak flooring, the mahogany furniture and cabinets, the white-tiled sinks and countertops. It was like going back in time.

Only, her childhood hadn't been happy. It had been filled with the frustration of growing up with a controlling mother. The house was bustling that night, full of guests.

"Patty, dear. I'm glad you're here. You look beautiful!" Her mother beamed, giving her a warm hug before her eyes darted to her daughter. Debbie didn't miss the way her face turned dark, the familiar disapproving look she'd given her almost all her life in full display for all to see.

"I don't think I can say the same to you, Debbie. What is that monstrosity you're wearing?"

Well, so much for staying calm throughout the party.

"I actually think it's stunning," Debbie spoke, emphasizing her words as she purposely moved her leg to show off skin from her slit, causing her mother to scowl at her.

"Red isn't a good color. It's too bold and confident, and men don't like bold and confident women. They prefer prim and proper, like white, or beige or like Patty's dress."

"That's good, mom. That's what I was going for. I don't like men, so I don't want them to like me." Debbie couldn't help but smirk slightly as she shrugged her shoulders. "I like red. My car is red. So, I think it's fitting for me to wear the color I like."

Her mom's frown deepened at her reply. "You having that car isn't a good choice either. I don't know why on earth you insisted on getting that atrocious red car." She paused, scrunching her nose before looking her up and down. "Red is the color harlots wear."

"Isn't that what you're doing? Prostituting me out to Craig?" Debbie replied nonchalantly, her mother giving her a horrified expression. *Being a parent doesn't mean you have the right to talk down to your children.*

"Okay, I-um, I think I want some food. I'm getting quite hungry, smelling the delicious feast from the kitchen. Show me the way, Debbie." Patty said in an attempt to diffuse the tension. Debbie visibly relaxed, exhaling silently before nodding.

"Please, excuse us." She told her mother, who kept her mouth shut against her clenched jaw.

They walked further into the house. Debbie looked around, desperately in search of the bar so she could get a drink. *Bingo.* She saw it and was drawn to it like a magnet, with Patty following her.

"Isn't it funny that your mom thinks you're dressed like a harlot, but also too confident to attract any men?" Patty teased. They stayed by the bar, Patty scanning the room for any potential men to talk to. Debbie had already downed one glass and was reaching for another.

"How many of these things do you think I could drink before I pass out?" She asked Patty. The only way she could get through her mother's parties was to drink. She didn't think anything could be worse than her mother's critical comments about her dress. Then Craig showed up.

"Debbie?"

A man's voice came from behind her, making both women turn to see Craig behind them. *Why are his glasses always crooked?* Before he had a chance to say much else, she heard another voice.

"Debbie?" It was like deja vu.

"Remember me? Randall? We went to high school together." He added, smiling charmingly at her, who looked too stunned to process what was happening. He was handsome and well-dressed. Patty took that opportunity to reach out a hand, batting her eyelashes at the man in a funny way while she smiled coyly.

"Hi, I'm Patty, Debbie's best friend."

Randall shook her hand, and she squeezed it lightly before giggling, although his attention was re-focused on the still speechless Debbie as soon as he let go of Patty's hand.

"So," the man started, finally getting Debbie out of her daydream, "How have you been? It's been a while since I last saw you."

"Oh. Well, yeah. I've been good." She laughed awkwardly, suddenly not knowing how to act. Craig was still hovering next to them. Debbie's cheeks turned pink.

"I'm Craig, Debbie's-"

"Do you still live in Crescent River?" Randall cut him off, causing Craig to glare at him.

"Yes... How did you know?" Debbie tilted her head, curious, while Randall chuckled, scratching his neck like he was embarrassed to say the reason he knew that.

"I've talked to your mother twice by coincidence, once when we crossed paths while I was here on a business trip, and the second was just a few days ago when she asked me to come to this party."

Patty glanced at her friend, who was now clearly blushing. She smirked, nudging her before smiling at Randall.

Patty asked, "So, you asked Debbie's mother about her?"

"Ah, it's nothing bad. I just wanted to catch up with my old friend from high school."

"You're still in a suit. Did you come here from work?" Debbie asked. He looked incredibly charming with his clean-cut hair and beard despite it having a few white strands here and there.

"I did, actually. I drove here from Ardor."

"Ardor?!" Patty exclaimed, genuinely surprised. "That's a long 4-hour drive from here. You must be so exhausted, then."

"You shouldn't have forced yourself to attend just to appease my mother," Debbie spoke, feeling guilty about having him here instead of letting him rest. Although, Randall was quick to assure her that it was no problem. Speaking of being nostalgic, seeing Randall brought Debbie back in time.

He was very amiable and handsome, rich and sophisticated, not to mention smart, the founder of his own company. Debbie hadn't seen him since he was a teenager. In those days, she had a huge crush on him.

Amidst the happy chatting of the three, Craig stood there almost fuming with irritation. He seemed jealous. *Maybe this party isn't so bad after all.* Debbie thought, enjoying her time catching up with Randall, who was more than happy to entertain her.

Just when Debbie was starting to have fun, an unexpected guest arrived at the party, wearing red and blue flannel over a white t-shirt, old-looking jeans, and leopard printed flip flops that had seen better days. His beard was long, and his hair had grown out. He stuck out like a sore thumb amongst the sea of well-dressed guests.

"It's Ed," Patty whispered to Debbie as if, somehow, she had forgotten about her oddball of a husband. Debbie just nodded, eyes stuck on the man in disbelief until she heard a gasp from somewhere nearby. It was Debbie's mother, mortified at seeing Ed.

"What do you think you're doing here?" She asked. "You're dressed like a logger." Her mother sneered, but Ed didn't seem to care nor feel offended by it.

He entered the house anyway, eyes darting around until he met Debbie's; she sucked in a breath. Ed stormed towards the four of them, grabbing Debbie's arm.

"Come one, let's get out of here." He said, "I need to talk to you. You need to be careful."

"Hey man, you're hurting her." Randall intervened, successfully pulling Debbie away from Ed since he saw how Debbie struggled to get away from Ed's tight grip on her upper arm. Ed glared at him.

"Stay out of this." He threatened, face growing darker, but Randall stood his ground.

"Look, Debbie doesn't want to go with you, so give it a rest. If you want to leave, then leave alone." Randall spoke, still polite, before ushering Debbie away, only to be stopped by Ed, who turned him around by the shoulder.

Ed asked, "Where do you think you're going with my wife?"

"Ed, please. Stop causing a scene." Debbie hissed, embarrassed by his actions

"Are you sleeping with this bastard? Is that why you want me to leave?" He asked.

Debbie's eyes widened, both because of what her husband had just said, but also because Ed went flying backward, knocking over a flower vase after Randall had punched his jaw. People stopped what they were doing to see the commotion. Not a single sound from the crowd could be heard as they waited for one of the men to make a move.

"You're a disgrace. A disgusting man and a worthless husband to accuse your wife of something so offensive, in a crowded place nonetheless." Randall said, face calm but voice clearly full of anger.

Ed stood up, wiping the small amount of blood from the corner of his busted lip while glaring at the man. Soon, a fistfight broke out, the two men throwing one punch after another as the crowd looked on. It was horrifying to Debbie.

"ENOUGH! BOTH OF YOU!" Debbie screamed, visibly ashamed of what had transpired before her. Randall quickly backed away, fixing his suit. Her husband's lip was busted, and a black eye was starting to form. Debbie made Ed leave, giving him no chance to speak another word as she was so disgusted that he would make a scene like that. Soon, the crowd dispersed, leaving only Randall, Debbie, and Patty to clean up the aftermath.

Bobo

After everything that happened, one thing was sure, Debbie was still obsessed with the case regarding Judy's murder. She just couldn't get over the fact that Ed was somehow mixed up in all of it. She decided to go to the cabin to gather information. But this time, she would go during the day.

She got in her red sedan and took off for the mountains. She drove by the graveyard again, unsure why she felt an eerie vibe there even when the sun was still shining. However, it was a little less creepy during the day.

The mountains were exquisite; the pine trees stood tall all year-round, glistening with raindrops during rainy seasons and covered in beautiful snow during winter. Debbie wished that she could live in the mountains. There was even a lake nearby where people could go fishing. It had a magnificent view, resembling a portrait.

She finally reached the cabin. It was quaint, with cedar shingles and logs on the sides giving it an old yet lovely look. Debbie liked the little porch swing the most since it reminded her of her children when they were young.

Why do I keep coming here? What do I expect to find?

There is nothing new in the cabin. All the evidence has been taken by the police. She still felt like there was something they might have missed. Then she realized that the neighbors might have been witnesses to something. She hadn't thought of that before.

The cabins weren't lined up together like houses in the city, but they were close enough to each other that a neighbor might have seen something. *I should ask the neighbors if they saw anything suspicious.*

She questioned the neighbors on both sides of the cabin, but none of them saw anything suspicious, or so they said. Feeling defeated, Debbie walked back to her car, freezing, when she heard something rustling in the bushes.

I hope it's not a bear, she thought. *Is it safe to move?* Debbie knew there were black bears in the area, although she had never encountered one. She turned around to see a man emerge from the bushes. He was dirty, and he smelled weird, his clothes tattered. His hair was wild and all over the place, uncut and unwashed.

"Hi, I'm Bobo," he said. "My name is actually Robert, but people call me Bobo. Well, not people, really. But animals..." He looked sheepishly at the ground. "Who are you?" He asked.

"Um... Debbie," she replied. "Can I ask you something, Bobo? Did you know anything about Judy's murder? The woman who lived here?"

"Yes, I know stuff about it," he said. He didn't look stable. "They're in the trees." He said, whispering with a crazed wide-eye look.

That's very confusing. Maybe I should go.

"I saw a man that night," Bobo continued. "A man with a gun."

"Could you identify the man if you saw him again?" She asked, shocked.

"I definitely could."

Debbie wished at that point that she had a picture of Philip, her number one suspect. Philip had pretended to be a drug dealer, but she didn't believe he was. Also, he threatened her right before Herman was found dead. Bobo had crazy eyes as Herman did.

Bobo continued on by telling her that he was listening outside the window the whole time. He heard the conversation. The man wanted the papers. And that confirmed something for Debbie.

This really is about the papers, whatever they are.

"They were talking about nuclear weapons, lasers, and chemical warfare, the sort of thing that could start World War III," Bobo said.

Maybe Bobo isn't crazy, Debbie thought. *That actually does make sense.*

"I already knew about World War III," he continued. "I had a dream about it. I'll be okay. I can hide in the trees."

Debbie looked at the ground. "Oh, that's a good idea," she said.

"They were talking about nuclear weapons, and the killer wanted Judy to tell him about them, but she refused, so he shot her."

Debbie was starting to piece things together; the articles she saw in Herman's room that time might've been related to what the man heard.

"There are people in the trees, I tell you. I have a mouse friend who speaks to me and told me the same story, so it's true." Debbie had believed him until that point.

"By the way, would you like to go out with me sometime? You're pretty." He continued.

Debbie squinted her eyes, "If we went out, where would we go?"

"There is a nice tree that I like to sit by and-"

"Oh, I'm sorry. I would, but I'm too busy right now. I'll have to take a rain check."

As Debbie drove home from the mountains that night, she thought about how weird it was that five men seemed to be interested in her, including her estranged husband. Just as she had decided that she hated men and wasn't looking for a relationship.

It had gotten foggy, and it was hard to see as she drove down the windy roads. Usually, she would be able to see the pine trees in the mountains, the crystal-clear moon, and the bright stars. But that night, she couldn't see much of anything at all. *It's just like my life, she thought. I don't understand anything. I can't see past the fog.*

She finally arrived home and went into her living room to get warm. The dampness of the night had made her cold to the bone. She grabbed a blanket and sat on her sofa, enveloping herself in its warmth. This room usually had a calming effect on her, making her want to curl up, relax, and shut out the world.

It was furnished with a plethora of cozy seats, a warm color scheme, plush fluffy pillows, soft blankets, and a fake fireplace to provide a cozy glow. But, tonight, it didn't make her feel calm at all. She was anything but calm. *What is wrong with Ed?* She thought. *I've never seen him act like that before. And could it be true what Bobo was saying? Could all of this really have to do with nuclear weapons? What has Ed gotten himself into? Does he know something he shouldn't know?*

The worst part was that she had no one to talk to about it except Fluffy, who didn't talk back. The weight of the world was on her shoulders. That's when she remembered the police officer, Matthew. He had told her that she could call him anytime if she needed help.

She looked at her contact list and stared at his name for a while. *Should I call him?* She thought. *Yes, Debbie,* she told herself, *you should definitely call him. You're in over your head.* She clicked on his number.

"Debbie?" A voice on the other end asked.

"Hi, Matthew." Her voice was shaky.

"Debbie? What's going on? Are you okay?" He seemed concerned.

"No, I'm not okay. Not really. There are some things I have to tell you, some developments you won't believe...."

Debbie was still trying to relax on her sofa but was unable to. *I'm not going to sleep tonight, not with all this on my mind.* She heard the phone ring, thinking it was Matthew calling back. *Does he know something?*

She answered and heard Ed's voice on the other end.

"Listen, Debbie; I'm really sorry for what happened at the party. I just, I got so jealous when I saw you with Randall and I lost it. I know that you had a crush on him in high school." He paused, hesitant. "Can we... Can we meet up? Let's have dinner together, my treat to make up for my behavior."

Debbie flared her nostrils, "Ed, what you did was really unfair. You hurt Randall. He didn't deserve to be treated like that. He didn't do anything wrong."

"I know, Deb, I don't know what got into me. I'm so sorry. Really. Genuinely."

He sounded sincere. But Debbie wanted to know more. "Ed, can you tell me what's going on?"

"No, I can't, Deb. I wish I could. But I can't. It's not safe." She was starting to believe him now.

Debbie wanted to see Ed. She was worried about him now and wanted to know if he was okay. "Alright," she said. "We'll meet."

"Meet me at the Pirates Café tomorrow night at 6."

The Pirate's Café? Debbie thought. *What a funny place to meet.* That had been the location of their first date.

ReDate

Debbie arrived at the restaurant and parked, noticing that Ed was standing in the front. He wasn't wearing his usual flannel but a nice button-up shirt and slacks. She noticed the quaint sign outside the restaurant, designed to look old. *Boy does this place bring back memories.*

They went into the restaurant and were seated. It was always loud in Pirate's Café since a large portion of it was a bar. There was a real tree growing in the restaurant, giving it a fairytale vibe. It had a vintage look with wines on display to choose from and small chandeliers hanging from the vaulted, dark mahogany ceiling. Debbie looked at the menu, which was also designed to look like it was from a different time. *Pesto bread, soup du jour, Ribs, Blue Champagne, chocolate pudding, ice cream. How can I possibly choose? Everything looks so good.*

Debbie couldn't think of what to say to her husband. "How is the Motel 6?" She asked.

"It's pretty nice, actually. There's a vending machine and a pool, although it's closed right now."

Motel 6 is nice? Really?

"Well, I'm glad you're happy there," Debbie replied, trying to be polite.

They didn't talk much during the meal. Once they were done, Ed paid the entire bill without letting Debbie see the price. She knew the meal was expensive. Ed then suggested that they go walking through town, to which Debbie agreed since it had been a while since she had enjoyed the company of her husband. The town was fairly quiet that night, a few night owls here and there and some cars rushing past. Debbie could see the mountains and trees from afar, remembering the old homeless man and his weird stories that sort of made sense.

"Do you remember the first time we met?" Ed asked at one point in the conversation as she nodded.

Debbie laughed softly. "The nuclear lab. You were trying to impress me but ended up making a fool of yourself."

"Well, first impressions last, huh? It worked, and you fell in love with me, even to the point of marrying a goofball like me."

That was true. She had loved him. She was starting to feel butterflies in her stomach.

As Debbie was pondering the good old days, she saw two men in suits staring at them from the other side of an alley they were passing. *Who are those men?* She thought. She was just beginning to feel that she might still be in love with Ed when one of the men pulled out a gun and started shooting at them.

Ed lay on the sidewalk, bleeding profusely. Debbie saw the red on the sidewalk and panicked.

"Ed! You've been shot!"

"It's fine. Just drive to the nearest hospital. I'll be fine, Debbie. It's just a scratch."

"It's not a scratch! You're bleeding!" She yelled back, assisting him to her car as gently as she could before driving him to the hospital. She was conflicted. *How could this sweet night turn into something so bitter?* Ed was admitted soon after they arrived at the emergency room.

"Excuse me, are you the patient's wife?" The doctor asked after a long time. Debbie quickly stood up, hands clammy in a nervous sweat and eyes shaky in worry.

"Yes. yes, I am."

"Your husband is safe now. Fortunately, the bullet missed his vital organs, and he just needed some minor stitching. He needs a lot of rest, so he will need to stay overnight."

"Can I go... Can I go visit my husband now?"

The doctor nodded with a smile. Debbie offered the doctor a grateful smile before rushing inside Ed's recovery room. He was awake and smiling.

"Thank goodness you're unharmed." He whispered, and Debbie couldn't help but feel that same feeling again. And, even though she was still mad at him, she felt bad that he had gotten himself caught up in this terrible thing. But most importantly, she felt truly relieved that Ed was alive and well.

Debbie's feet moved on their own as she walked closer and closer to him. She was staring deep into his eyes, hearing her own heart through her eardrums as she leaned over and kissed him on the lips.

It had been a few days since the incident, and Debbie still couldn't sleep. It wasn't entirely because she and Ed had been targeted while together or that Ed could've died in her presence. It was also partially because of how impulsive and idiotic she had been, suddenly kissing her husband on the lips despite the awkwardness and uncertainty of their relationship. It didn't mean anything other than a rush of emotion, although Debbie would be lying if she said she didn't miss Ed's lips. They were chapped and dry that night, but they never failed to make her feel warm inside.

Debbie unconsciously touched her lips, lying on her bed while staring blankly at the ceiling. She let her mind wander a bit more, reminiscing of the days when kissing her husband wasn't so conflicting, back when they were happy, if they ever were truly happy. She sighed, flopping her hand on the mattress before closing her eyes.

Why am I thinking about this? This isn't the time to be thinking about a relationship. I have a murder to solve, a killer to find. I have to find out the truth about what's going on. I have no time to rekindle silly emotions for a man I can't even trust.

It hurt to feel that way and to acknowledge that she couldn't trust her husband. She wanted to trust him with her whole heart. Sadly, Ed still wouldn't tell her the truth.

She sighed once more, this time sighing a little longer. She was exhausted. Fluffy jumped on the bed to cuddle her as if sympathizing with his stressed-out owner. Debbie was thankful for her companion, petting the fluffball in adoration as she appreciated the momentary silence while they cuddled. As soon as she started falling asleep, her phone rang.

Grumbling, she stretched her arms out, eyes still closed as she blindly searched for her phone, remembering that she had placed it on the bedside table.

I should've put the freaking phone on silent. She finally opened her eyes to look for her phone properly. Once she saw the blaring gadget, she grabbed it roughly, answering it, without even glancing at the screen to see who was calling.

"Hello?" she spoke a little harshly.

"Is that a way to answer your mother's call?"

Great. Just great.

"Mom... It's almost midnight. Why are you calling me so late?"

Debbie's mom muttered gibberish she couldn't understand. She talked for a while as if she was doing a monologue in a play before suddenly opening up a very unwanted topic.

"Have you been keeping in touch with Craig?"

Of course not. Why would I? I don't even have the man's number, was what she wanted to say.

"I haven't been keeping in touch with many people," was her safe reply. She could hear a disapproving huff, followed by a lighter tone of voice.

"I need you to go with Craig to lunch tomorrow." She started, making Debbie sit up on her bed suddenly wide-eyed, scaring poor Fluffy away.

"What?" she spat out, flabbergasted by her mother's sudden demand.

"I said I need you to go with Craig tomorrow for lun...."

"No, mom, I'm not taking Craig to lunch. It was bad enough I had to spend the evening with him at the party." She interfered, resolute to her unwavering dislike for the man.

"Craig doesn't know that many people here." Debbie's mother tried to reason out, a lame excuse, Debbie felt.

"Still a no, mom. If you want, you can do it instead since you like him so much."

She could tell her mother was scowling even through the phone. "What do you have against Craig? He's a good man."

"He's boring, mom. He's really not fun to be with at all. I'd probably enjoy talking to a wall more than talking to him. Or staying home with Fluffy."

"He's not boring, Debbie. What you call boring, I call stable. Craig is intelligent, hard-working, and he's going places." Her mother corrected. She rolled her eyes dramatically, letting slip a sarcastic remark to express her annoyance.

Debbie said, "Mom, did it ever occur to you that I have things to do? Did you ever think that maybe there are things on my mind?"

"No, what could you possibly have to do? Your husband isn't even there. You only have to cook for one."

"I have a friend who was... murdered. I'm trying to figure out who did it." She replied.

"Don't investigate that case, Deborah. That sounds dangerous. Leave it to the police." Her mom said in a panicky tone.

"I'm hanging up now, mom. Goodbye."

"Deb-" Debbie's mom's voice cut off as she hung up. She carelessly let her phone drop on the bed as she flopped back onto the comfort of her mattress. She blinked once or twice before rolling to her side and succumbing to sleep, far too tired for her brain to function.

Debbie woke up the next day with a grumbling tummy, joking to herself about how her stress was causing her to binge-eat. Still a little groggy due to her lack of sleep because of her mother's nonsensical call, she went into the kitchen searching for something to satisfy her hunger. She opened her fridge with a bit more force than usual, her stomach growling in sync. Alas, all there was were some vegetables and old milk. That didn't seem very appealing. Debbie looked in the freezer as well, grimacing at the single untouched tub of chocolate ice cream. It was practically screaming, *eat me.*

Darn. I've told myself that I'm going to stop eating ice cream.

"Oh well. I'll give it up another time." Debbie shrugged, taking the tub of tempting dessert out of the freezer. "I'll stop tomorrow."

She brought it back to the dining room and started eating it out of the tub. She took a spoonful of the sugary stuff, wincing at the coldness before finally savoring the taste.

Interesting breakfast, her mind couldn't help but snark as she continued eating. Just then, her phone rang again. This time, she looked at it to see who it was, but she didn't recognize the number.

Who could be calling me this early? It could be anyone: mom, Ed, the killer.

Debbie gulped, suddenly feeling more vigilant about the mysterious caller.

"Hello?" she warily asked.

"Hi, Deb, it's so good to hear your voice. How are you?"

The voice sounded familiar, but she couldn't place it. "Who is this?" She questioned.

"It's me, Craig." *Oh my gosh, Craig.*

"Wait, how did you get my number?"

The voice chuckled arrogantly, "Your mom told me that you were too shy to tell me that you want me to take you out to lunch."

"Oh, my mom said that, did she?"

"Yeah, she did. I find it silly but adorable. You know you don't have to be shy around me. I'd love to take you out for a date."

"Wow. Lovely." Debbie was trying her best to sound as polite as she could. It would've been fine if Craig wasn't so arrogant, clingy, or dull. They could've been acquaintances if her mother wasn't pushing him on her. Poor Craig seemed to be oblivious to the fact that she wasn't interested in him.

"So, where do you want to go?" He asked.

"You see, the thing is, Craig...." *The thing is that I find you boring. I don't enjoy your company. I don't like you. You don't have a chance with me.*

"Yes, Debbie?"

"The thing is... I'd love to go to lunch with you." *What's wrong with me? Why did I say that?* Debbie had a difficult time being direct; no matter how annoyed and sarcastic she could get.

"Oh wow, really?! Great! I'll send you the location. See you later, Deb!" She cringed at the nickname, sighing after he had ended the call.

"Wonderful. Now I have to go and meet Craig. Yay, me." Debbie berated herself for not being able to say no when she didn't want to do something. She had to think of some way to let him know she wasn't interested so he wouldn't follow her around for the rest of their lives. But, at that moment, she just couldn't disappoint him.

Yet Another Date

Hours had passed since Debbie had been at work, and nothing had happened. *What a boring day*, she thought. She stared out at the vineyard. There were rows and rows of grapes; the purple-skinned white-fleshed berries grew in clusters on wooden structures to keep them off the ground. Usually, she loved looking out at the vineyard.

But that day, she wasn't enjoying anything. *I should be trying to solve Judy's murder, figuring out what's going on with Ed, and figuring out if I really have those papers*. And now she had to go to lunch with Craig. *Maybe I should just not show up?*

She drove to the restaurant full of dread. It was called Peter's Deli, a simple shop that mainly sold sandwiches. The drive didn't take long. After all, it was a small town. The restaurant was actually in a lovely location. It stood on top of a road extension that was built on a hill with an ocean view.

Well, I might as well eat a lot. Good food is good food, after all. And there's nothing in my fridge. She told herself as she walked inside the restaurant. Its interior was an intriguingly beautiful mix of golden-yellow, orange, off-white, and powder blue with wood ceiling, floors, and tables.

The windows were large and wide to give customers a good view while eating. It didn't take long for Craig to spot her, waving a hand animatedly at her with the biggest smile.

"You came." He said, try to act cool. *Wasn't he acting like a kid a few seconds ago?*

"Yeah... Have you been waiting for long?"

"Not at all. I just arrived as well."

They sat down at a table and ordered sandwiches. "You seem a little preoccupied," Craig said. "Is everything okay?"

"Actually, no, it's not. My friend was," she paused, "murdered. I'm trying to figure out who killed her," she said in a serious tone.

"I could help you with that." He offered.

"How could you help me?"

"I know a lot about murder."

"Like what?"

"Like In 2017, it was recorded that 464,000 people were killed intentionally... Also, in 2017, reports stated that the worldwide murder rate was 6.1 victims per 100,000 people. Male criminals were responsible for almost 90% of all murders that were reported over the globe. Nearly 80% of all murder victims in the world's records are male."

"That doesn't help me," Debbie said, disappointed. *It's like talking to a computer*. Debbie finished her food first. "Hey Craig, I need to go back to work." She said, preparing to leave as the man chowed down the remaining food on his plate, almost choking halfway through.

"W-wait," he choked, coughing before chugging down his drink. "I'll drive you there."

"It's fine. I got here using my car."

"I know. I'm saying I'll drive your car and take you to work. I also want to know where it is."

Oh no. Not a chance.

"It's fine, really. I also need to drive somewhere before going there."

"No, no. I insist."

"Craig, really please, I need to... I need to go buy some pads. So, I don't really want you going with me since it's embarrassing." She just said anything she could think of as the man blushed. *It always works to mention your period. Men are terrified of it, even though I don't get periods anymore since I've started menopause.*

"O-oh. Okay."

"Yeah, so. Ha-ha. Bye. Thanks for lunch, by the way." They both stood up. Before she could move away, Craig threw his arms around her and kissed her forehead. Debbie blinked at the blushing man as he backed away.

"I... I'm so sorry." He said, sounding genuine as he looked down in shame. "I just... I thought you looked beautiful and that I wouldn't have another chance to do that...." Craig then looked up, eyes hopeful, at Debbie. "Or not... If you give me a chance, Debbie."

"No." She breathed out, a surge of air rising to her throat as if she'd been under water. "I'm sorry. I really need to go."

Before Craig could utter another word, Debbie bolted out of the restaurant, not even looking back at the confused and dejected man.

When Debbie finally got home that evening, she tried her best to think of anything but Craig and their weird outing. Her mind wandered off to Bobo and the strange things he had said to her. After all, Ed had worked at the nuclear lab, and so had Herman and Judy, who were both now deceased. Plus, Herman had all those clippings from newspaper articles where he circled words like nuclear, chemical weapons, and lasers. Incidentally, that's what Bobo was talking about. She'd almost believed him until he'd mentioned the mouse.

"I still don't get it." She said to Fluffy as she fed him. "I don't know what those mysterious papers could be."

Debbie decided to search her house yet again just to double-check and to busy her mind. She looked in every box she had, in every drawer, but it still didn't make sense. Most of the "papers" she had were bills.

She found nothing. Not really knowing what to do, she spent some time playing with Fluffy. If only Ed could've been more open and honest with her, she would've walked on burning coals to help him out of this mess he'd gotten himself into.

Shaking her head, she tried to dismiss those thoughts. Debbie had been trying not to think about her relationship with Ed for the longest time. It was too complicated to put into words. She didn't understand how she felt. She put it out of her mind, and, instantly, her thoughts turned to Craig instead. *Oh no, I don't want to think about Craig. That's even worse.* Then a light bulb went on in her brain. She started thinking about something Craig had said to her. Most murderers were men. That's interesting. This whole time she had felt there was a big conspiracy going on involving weapons of mass destruction and spies. Maybe it was something much simpler than that. Perhaps it had simply been a matter of testosterone. Maybe a man had done it, a man who was a little crazy, a man like Bobo. He was there that night, and he lived in the forest nearby.

She realized she had to go back to the cabin and question Bobo again. *Maybe he would confess.* She got in her car and headed for the mountain. Every time she drove by that same graveyard, she shuttered. *Why am I so freaked out by that place?*

As she waited on the porch of Judy's cabin, she heard him muttering to himself, looking up in the trees. Debbie shivered, her skin crawling at the thought that he might be a murderer. *Be careful, Debbie. Don't provoke him.* Bobo then snapped his head toward Debbie, so quickly, in fact, that it caused Debbie to flinch.

"Who's there? Are you one of them?" He called out, wild eyes moving left and right. Debbie opted to reveal herself, observing the way Bobo's eyes stayed on her as she slowly walked down the porch steps and toward him.

"You're back!" He said in glee, but Debbie shot him an interrogating glare.

"I'm not here to flirt, Bobo. What were you doing the night of the murder?"

"Me? I was with my mouse friend. We were hiding from the people in the trees." Bobo explained, making creepy gestures and odd facial expressions.

Debbie didn't buy his story. "Stop lying and tell me where you were that night."

"I'm not lying! I don't lie! My mouse friend, he told me to hide away from the people. You can talk to him, my mouse friend. He would be happy to meet you! Let's go! Let's go! I'll point you to...."

"Stop dilly-dallying and just tell me the truth before I call the police!" She warned, taking her phone out of her pocket to show Bobo that she wasn't messing around. Bobo stared at her for a minute, silent and unmoving, until he shook his head vehemently. He started talking to himself again, a little more aggressively than before.

"Should I tell her or not?" He asked himself. "Lies are bad. Wolves in sheep's clothing are bad." He continued mumbling for a while.

"Answer me, gosh darn it!" She shouted angrily, scaring the homeless man who crouched into a ball. When she still didn't get the answer she wanted, she dialed 9-1-1. "I'm here with a possible murder suspect," she told the operator.

The police arrived in five minutes and surrounded Bobo, who stood up immediately, shouting, "They're watching us from satellites! Nuclear war is coming! It's coming! It's coming! I didn't mean to kill her. It was an accident." The police handcuffed Bobo, reading him his rights and taking him away.

Debbie was relieved that the murderer had finally been arrested. Maybe she could finally get some sleep. Maybe things could finally go back to normal. But she had no peace of mind at all. She felt like she kept seeing things in her peripheral vision. At first, she thought it was Bobo's paranoia. *War is coming. They're watching us from satellites.* Could it be?

As days turned into nights, she was certain something was wrong. She felt like someone was following her. She thought of the night Ed had nearly died. *Someone shot at him. Why?* She was becoming more and more anxious. She decided not to leave the house and asked her boss, Al, for sick leave, saying that she had the flu and was very contagious; he allowed her the time off.

She wanted this case to be over more than anything before she completely lost her mind. Debbie didn't want anyone else getting hurt. She kept seeing a man parked outside her driveway in the evenings. He never tried to approach her or talk to her. He just sat outside in a car that was parked on her street. *No one ever parks on this street.*

Maybe the case isn't closed after all. Maybe Bobo had been a decoy, so she would let her guard down before an attack. She couldn't bear the burden anymore, so she called Matthew.

"I think someone is following me," she said to the detective. "Usually, in the evening, a man parks outside my house."

"Really? I wouldn't worry about it," Matthew said. "It's probably just a friend of your neighbor."

"Did you hear about Bobo getting arrested?" She asked.

"Yes, I heard. But I don't think he is the killer."

"Why not?" She asked.

"No motive. Truthfully, I don't want to be the one to tell you this. But, be careful around your husband. I don't trust the man. Right now, he is our number one suspect."

"What? Ed? No way, Ed would never kill anyone. He may be eccentric, but he's no murderer." She said.

"Just promise you'll be careful," Matthew reiterated and hung up.

Nibbling on her lower lip, she looked through the window. The car was still there. It hadn't moved an inch. *Ed, a murderer? That doesn't make any sense. I should go and talk to him, she thought. I should go now.*

Will the man follow me if I go somewhere? She asked inwardly, weighing the pros and cons of leaving the house. The pros were that she could go to Ed's motel room and ask him directly and tell him what was going on. Perhaps he would finally tell her what he knew. She could also lose the car that was following her along the way. That way, the man wouldn't know if she had returned home or not since she could leave her sedan at the motel or somewhere else in the meantime. There were no cons, except that Ed was a suspect. She didn't feel safe in her home. She needed to be near Ed. He was her husband, after all, and he was a lot of things but he was no murderer.

"Shoot. What should I do?" She was losing time now. If she didn't decide on something, she might regret it. "Heck with it." She cursed, taking her car keys and turning the front doorknob. She swung the door, trembling as she tried to remain unfazed by this risky situation. One wrong move, and she may never see another day.

She drove off, every so often looking in her mirrors to see if the other car was tailing her.

Is this how Judy felt? Is this why Herman secluded himself from society? Is this why Ed has become so distant and unrecognizable? Debbie felt that all their paranoia was suddenly justifiable.

She arrived at Ed's motel room in one piece and unscathed. Looking for something to protect herself in case things escalated, she grabbed the pen she had in her car and pocketed it.

"For safety measures." She assured herself as she exited the car, looking in every direction to see if she had been followed.

"Did I lose him?" Debbie mumbled, entering the building, where she was truly at a loss for words. The motel had grabbed her attention, but not in a good way — its walls were beige, but the doors were bright blue. It was plain-looking. She couldn't believe that Ed had chosen to stay there instead of at home with her.

"What are you doing here?" was Ed's greeting, leaning forward to look around the hall before pulling Debbie inside his room. "You're not supposed to be here."

She almost felt sorry for the man when she saw the state of the room he had been living in for the past couple of months. Ed was never good at keeping things neat; Debbie was the neat one. His clothes were everywhere, the dirty ones appearing to be mixed in with the clean ones, all of them thrown haphazardly around. It was weird for her to see him living like this. So painful that he chose to live in this mess instead of the comfort of their home.

"Are you aware that I'm being followed?" She asked, closing the door behind her.

"What?" Ed asked. Debbie could tell that he was surprised by her statement.

Debbie continued. "Someone has been stalking me for a week now. I thought I got the killer, but I don't know anymore."

Ed's demeanor changed, panic in his eyes as he paced around the room. Debbie took that moment to take in the full view of his room; one of the walls was painted orange, which was peculiar. There were stacks of empty and crushed beer cans in one of the corners alongside some pizza boxes and take-out bags. However, what caught her attention was the stack of papers on his mini table. She was a hundred percent sure her husband knew something that she didn't.

"I went on a date...." She started off, noticing how he stopped his pacing. "With Craig."

Ed looked at her, his face a mixture of confusion and agitation. "Why are you telling me this now? To make me jealous?"

"No." Debbie sat on the bed, eyes glued on him while the two wall lamps illuminated their features warmly, their orange hues opposing the way she was feeling. "I'm telling you this because I want to be honest." She sighed as she continued. "I want us to be honest, Ed. Just once, I want to know what's bothering you."

"I can't."

"What? Why can't you? Was having a relationship with me not enough? Was being married to me for so many years, building our own family, not enough for you to trust me?"

"Debbie, it's not that easy."

"That's bull, Ed." She spat. Unbeknownst to her, she was shaking her fist and quivering her lips as she stared at him, knowing he was lying to her. "I know it's difficult for you to be honest. I never said it was easy. But I'm asking you to confide in me, as your wife, as a member of your family. Ed, I'm your other half. I vowed to you the day we got married. You vowed to me...."

Debbie was sniffling at that point but held her tears back as Ed remained silent. She stood up and walked closer to him, taking both his cold hands in hers.

"Give me one chance to be your confidant, Ed. Trust me, just this once."

"I... I'm sorry, Debbie." He spoke, pulling his hands away from hers just as he kept removing himself from her life. Debbie almost broke down right then and there as Ed walked into the bathroom and closed the door. She was left alone, heart and soul laid bare before him, but she still couldn't reach his heart.

She could only laugh in sadness, so sad that she couldn't stop the tears. *I knew it would be this way, so why do I still feel like my heart's shattering into pieces?*

Debbie looked at the closed bathroom door once more before deciding to leave, she turned for the door tripping on some clothes on the floor and accidentally pulling one of his drawers open. Luckily for her, there were some clothes on the floor, although a little funny smelling, that saved her from getting a concussion or bad bruise.

"Ouch." Debbie winced, pushing herself up as she felt something cold and solid under her hand. Confused, she raised her hand to see what it was as the bathroom door swung open.

"Goodness, Debbie, are you oka-"

Ed hadn't finished his sentence when Debbie picked up the cold thing in her hand before looking at him with fear and bewilderment. She raised the thing for him to get a better view. It had fallen out of the bottom of his sock drawer.

"Debbie, let's remain calm and hand it over to me-"

"Ed...Why do you have a gun with you?"

Did you enjoy this book?

If so, please leave a review on Amazon!

https://www.amazon.com/review/create-review/?ie=UTF8&channel=glance-detail&asin=B0B5SF6FN6

Ready for more? Follow this and other favorites below!

https://www.ttpublishinghouse.com/legendsreborn

https://www.ttpublishinghouse.com/7wishes

https://www.ttpublishinghouse.com/mallcadet

www.ingramcontent.com/pod-product-compliance
Lightning Source LLC
Chambersburg PA
CBHW071952120726
48001CB00005B/2147

9798841145448